I bet you are wondering ...
You are? I thought so!
When one sock goes missing,
where on earth does it go?

Well, this tale is quite something,
I mean it, it's true,
if you find just one sock,
when before there were two.

Icky and grungy these creatures are not,
though they live under the floorboards
with the dust and the grot.

Sock Pixies, they're called,
and they live in your house.

These shy, little sprites
ride on top of a mouse!

They run and they scamper across your bedroom.

To find what they're after, in the deep sock drawer gloom.

Be they holey or smelly, Sock Pixies don't mind.

They love all of our footgloves, and will take what they find.

They weave and they knit,
all the socks that they took ...

... they're doing it now, while
you're reading this book!

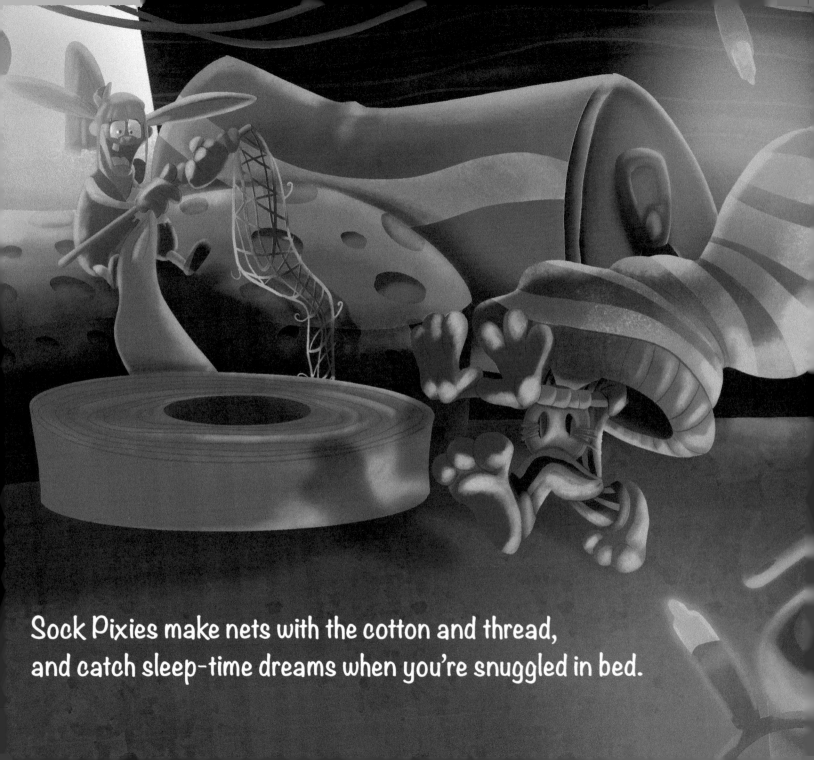

Sock Pixies make nets with the cotton and thread,
and catch sleep-time dreams when you're snuggled in bed.

On the backs of their
mice, while you sleep
safe and still,

the Sock Pixies gather
on your big windowsill.

They swoop and they swipe
with the nets they have made,

catching all of the dreams on
their night-time dream raid.

The nice ones they bag
and drop into your ear.

But the bad ones they eat, gobbled up with a beer!

See, the Sock Pixies want you to sleep well in bed,
so they pop only lovely dreams into your head.

Remember those
pixies living way
down below.

They find you sweet dreams, taking good care of you.

Which is why,
when you look ...

... there's just one sock
– not two!

The Hubble & Hattie imprint was launched in 2009, and is named in memory of two very special Westie sisters owned by Veloce's proprietors. Since the first book, many more have been added, all with the same objective: to be of real benefit to the species they cover, at the same time promoting compassion, understanding and respect between all animals (including human ones!)

Our new range of books for kids will champion the same values and standards that we've always held dear, but to the adults of the future. Children will love reading, or having read to them, these beautifully illustrated, carefully crafted publications, absorbing valuable life lessons whilst being highly entertained. We've more great books already in the pipeline so remember to check out our website for details.

Other great books from our Hubble & Hattie Kids! imprint

 9781787116993

 9781787115163

 9781787113060

 9781787113121

 9781787114180

 9781787114302

 9781787117464

 9781787111608

 9781787112926

 9781787115156

 9781787113077

 9781787113862

 9781787117631

 9781787117792

 9781787117389

 9781787117198

 9781787117488

 9781787117372

 9781787117730

www.hubbleandhattie.com/hubbleandhattiekids/

First published June 2022 by Veloce Publishing Limited, Veloce House, Parkway Farm Business Park, Middle Farm Way, Poundbury, Dorchester, Dorset, DT1 3AR, England. Tel: 01305 260068/Fax: 01305 250479 Email: info@hubbleandhattie.com/web www.hubbleandhattie.com ISBN: 978-1-787117-79-2 UPC:6-36847-01779-8 © Jim Crawley & Veloce Publishing Ltd 2022. All rights reserved.
British Library Cataloguing in Publication Data: a catalogue record for this book is available from the British Library. Typesetting, design and page make-up all by Veloce Publishing Ltd on Apple Mac. Printed and bound by CPI Group (UK) Ltd, Croydon CR0 4YY